MATT CHRISTOPHER®

#7
WILD RIDE

Text by Stephanie Peters
Illustrated by Michael Koelsch

LITTLE, BROWN AND COMPANY

New York ᔧ Boston

Little, Brown and Company

Time Warner Book Group
1271 Avenue of the Americas, New York, NY 10020
Visit our Web site at www.lb-kids.com

www.mattchristopher.com

First Edition

Library of Congress Cataloging-in-Publication Data
Peters, Stephanie True.
Wild ride / Matt Christopher ; text by Stephanie Peters ;
illustrated by Michael Koelsch. — 1st ed.
p.   cm. — (The extreme team ; #7)
Summary: Knowing that the mountain trails are unsafe for bicycles
due to fallen trees and other obstacles, Jonas helps organize
a clean-up crew in early spring, but when he hears someone
else biking on the trail he cannot resist a ride of his own.
ISBN 0-316-76263-6 (pb) / ISBN 0-316-76262-8 (hc)
[1. All terrain cycling — Fiction.   2. Bicycles and bicycling —
Fiction.   3. Safety — Fiction.]   I. Christopher, Matt.
II. Koelsch, Michael, ill.   III. Title.   IV. Series.
PZ7.P441833Wi 2005   2003023760
[Fic] — dc22

10   9   8   7   6   5   4   3   2   1

PHX (hc)

COM-MO (pb)

Printed in the United States of America

CHAPTER ONE

Jonas Malloy blew on his icy fingertips and rubbed his hands together. Despite the bright April-morning sunshine pouring through a window, it was cold inside the Malloys' garage. But Jonas didn't care. He was busy cleaning his mountain bike to get it ready for the first ride of the season.

"'Bout time you came out of hibernation," he said to his bike as he squatted down next to it. Arranged on the floor beside him were some clean rags, a pair of rubber gloves, a small bottle of bike-chain lubricant, and a dry paintbrush. He selected the brush first. Starting at one end, he used it to flick a winter's worth of dust and dirt from the frame and wheels.

"Want to tackle my bike next?"

Jonas looked over his shoulder. His father stood in the doorway, a big grin on his face.

Jonas jerked a thumb to where his dad's bike leaned against the wall. "Already took care of it. Anything to get us out on the trails sooner!"

Mr. Malloy's grin faded. "Jonas, I know you're anxious to do some biking. But even though you and the bikes are ready, the trails might not be. You know my rule: Until the trails are safe, no riding."

Jonas spun the bike's back wheel. "I know," he mumbled.

"Course, that doesn't mean we can't ride *to* the trails," his father continued with a smile. "How about we ride over after lunch and take a hike up the mountain to check things out?"

Jonas's eyes lit up. "That'd be great!" he replied. "Thanks, Dad." He held up the paintbrush. "Meantime, I'll keep cleaning my bike."

Mr. Malloy nodded and returned to the house. Jonas turned his attention back to his bike. He went

over every inch of it with the brush. Then he rubbed it all over with a dry rag to remove any last specks of dirt the brush had missed.

"Now for the chain," he said. He flipped the bike over and balanced it on its handlebars and seat. After pulling on a pair of rubber gloves, he picked up another soft, clean cloth and draped it over a section of chain. Holding the cloth-covered chain with one hand, he turned the pedals with the other to make the chain move. After a few turns, the cloth had cleaned the outside of the entire chain.

Then he picked up the bottle of lubricant. Working slowly and carefully, he applied the thick, black liquid to each link. He waited a few minutes, then once again ran the chain through the cloth. When he was done, the chain was clean and freshly oiled.

Jonas flipped the bike over, leaned it against the garage wall, and stood back to admire his work. The bike shone like new. As he began to pick up his cleaning supplies, he couldn't help but grin.

I can hardly wait to get it muddy again!

CHAPTER TWO

After lunch, Jonas and his father set off for the mountain.

"Your bike working okay?" Mr. Malloy asked as they rode along.

"Running as smooth as a fruit smoothie!" Jonas joked.

"Mine, too. Thanks for getting it ready."

Fifteen minutes later, they rode into a parking lot at the base of a small mountain. On the other side of the mountain was the cleared-off slope where Jonas and his friends went snowboarding during the winter. On this side of the mountain, trails had been cut in and around the trees and boulders. Some trails were just for hikers. Others were marked for mountain bikers. Every so often the two types of trails intersected. These intersections were marked clearly so hikers and bikers could be on the lookout and avoid collisions.

"Well," Mr. Malloy said, "let's go take a look." He locked up his bike, shouldered a backpack, and started up a hiking trail. Jonas was right behind him.

It was only the first week of April. A few trees had leaf buds on them, but most were bare. On the ground, unseen creatures scurried through beds of old leaves. Jonas heard a bird call from above and craned his neck to look for it.

Whump!

"Oof!" Mr. Malloy grunted.

"Sorry, Dad!" Mr. Malloy had stopped suddenly, and Jonas had walked smack into him.

"No problem," Mr. Malloy said. "Or, actually, I should say small problem. Look up ahead."

The trail in front of them was completely blocked by a fallen tree. Branches stuck up every which way, making it impossible to climb over the trunk.

"We'll have to go around," Mr. Malloy said. "Follow me."

They stepped off the path and began to pick their way carefully through a tangle of old brush. Prickers grabbed at Jonas's pants, forcing him to stop and pull them free. Two steps later, his foot sank into a mire of swampy mud. There was a wet sucking sound when he yanked it out. Mr. Malloy wasn't having an easy time of it, either. "Drat!" he muttered as he tripped over a tree root.

Finally, they made it around the fallen tree and back to the trail. But even then it was slow going. Winter had taken its toll, filling the path with tree branches. Snowmelt had left huge puddles of water and mud in the hollows. They even came across a pile of rocks from a rock slide. After twenty minutes, Mr. Malloy took off the backpack and leaned against a boulder.

"Whew!" he said. "This trail is in rough shape!" He handed Jonas a water bottle, then took a swig from his own. "And I'll bet the other trails are just as bad."

Jonas almost choked mid-swallow. He had a sneaking suspicion that his dad was about to say something he didn't want to hear. He was right.

"Jonas, I'm afraid that until these trails are cleared, there'll be no biking. Sorry, pal." He stood up, shouldered the pack again, and began to head back down the trail.

Jonas knew his father was only thinking about his safety. And he knew it would be risky to bike in such conditions. But still, as he followed his father down the mountain and to their bikes, disappointment ran through his veins.

If only there were something I could do, he thought as they rode out of the lot.

They were halfway home when he realized there *was* something he could do.

"Dad!" he yelled. "Turn around! Quick!"

CHAPTER THREE

Mr. Malloy braked sharply. "What is it? Are you hurt?"

"No," Jonas replied. "We need to go to the Community Center so I can talk to Alison. Please?"

The Community Center ran the local skatepark in the spring, summer, and fall, and then the slope in the winter. Alison Lee, the teenager who oversaw both the skatepark and the slope, was so into extreme sports that Jonas was sure she'd be willing to help him.

Five minutes later, they pulled up in front of the center. Jonas hurried inside, followed closely by his father. He spotted Alison behind the front desk.

"Yo, Malloys, what's up?" Alison greeted them.

Jonas told her about the impassable trails. "So what I was hoping," he finished, "was that you'd help me figure out a way to get the trails ready for biking. And hiking, too, of course," he added.

Alison drummed her fingers on the desktop. "Funny you should ask. I've been planning to organize a clean-up day for those trails. From what you've said, it sounds like we're going to need a big crew."

Her eyes flicked toward a wall calendar. "Hmm. The skatepark opens next Saturday. I'll be too busy to do anything that day" — Jonas's heart started to sink — "so how about the day after?"

Jonas's heart leapt up again.

"Tell you what," Alison said, "if you find enough people willing to put in a full day of hard work next Sunday, I'll be there to show them what needs to be done. Just make sure everyone wears pants and long sleeves and has a pair of heavy-duty work gloves. Think you can do that?"

"Absolutely!" Jonas cried. "Thanks, Alison!"

She waved a hand. "No sweat, kid. In the meantime, I'll post a sign warning people to stay off the trails."

The minute Jonas got home, he started calling his friends.

"X, ol' buddy, ol' friend, ol' pal!" he said when Xavier "X" McSweeney answered his phone.

"Uh, oh," X replied. "What's with the buddy-friend-pal stuff? You must want something."

Jonas filled him in. X readily agreed to help with the cleanup.

"I'll ask my mom, too. She loves all that outdoorsy stuff."

"Excellent! And call Savannah and Charlie, would you?" Jonas said. Their friends Savannah Smith and Charlie Abbott were also into extreme sports. "I'll call Bizz and Mark."

Belicia "Bizz" Juarez and Mark Goldstein promised to lend a hand that Sunday. Both said they'd ask their parents to join them. Jonas left a message at the Community Center telling Alison he'd rounded up a crew. He was still smiling when he hung up the phone.

Now if I can just put mountain biking out of my mind for the next week, I'll be all set!

CHAPTER FOUR

Luckily, the following week was a busy one for Jonas. Besides going to school every day and doing his homework at night, he had to get his inline skates and skateboard ready for the grand reopening of the skatepark on Saturday.

Good thing I already took care of my bike! he thought as he tightened the trucks on his board with a wrench.

Saturday morning was bright and sunny. Jonas hurried through breakfast, filled a water bottle, grabbed some snacks, then found his father to tell him he was heading for the skatepark.

Mr. Malloy swiveled around in his office chair. "I'll be out most of the day. Can you fix your own lunch?" When Jonas nodded, he added, "Oh, I'm going to leave you a list of chores to do when you get back. I'll be home by three. Have them done by then, okay?"

"You bet!"

In the garage, Jonas debated whether to skate or board to the park. When a shaft of sunlight glinted off his bike, however, he decided to ride instead.

"I should take it for another test drive to be absolutely, positively certain it's all in order," he said to himself. He shoved his water bottle into its carrier on the bike's frame and put his inline skates and safety gear into his backpack.

The pavement zipped along beneath him as his legs pumped the pedals. At the end of his street, he gave the hand brakes a gentle squeeze. To his left was the road that would take him to the skatepark. If he went right, he'd be on the road to the mountain trails.

He looked up the right side of the street wistfully.

Soon, he reminded himself, and turned toward the skatepark.

When he arrived, a small crowd had gathered at the front entrance. Jonas was locking up his bike when a hand slapped him on the back.

"Your ride is looking primo, Jo!" X said, eyeing the bike. "Maybe a little cleaner than I'm used to seeing it, though."

Jonas grinned. "No kidding. If that bike doesn't see mud soon, it's going to go crazy!"

Mark, Bizz, and Charlie appeared a moment later. Charlie and Bizz were wearing their inlines. Mark was carrying his and rubbing his elbow.

"Why don't you put those on?" X asked, pointing to his skates.

"I did have them on," Mark admitted. "But I took a little spill, so I figured I had better take them off until I got here."

"Where'd you fall?" Bizz wanted to know.

Mark looked sheepish. "In my driveway. Guess I'm a little rusty."

X threw an arm around his shoulders. "Don't worry, it'll all come back to you. Once you know how, inline skating is as easy as falling off a log!"

Mark winced. "Did you have to mention 'falling'?"

Their laughter was interrupted by the sound of Alison's voice. "Okay, everybody, this is it. The moment you've been waiting all winter for!" She unlocked the skatepark gate and swung the door wide open. "Let the extreme sports of spring begin!"

Jonas and the others gave a *whoop.* With one last glance at his bike to make sure it was locked tight, he made his way to a bench and took his pads and skates out of his backpack. He quickly traded his sneakers for his inlines, strapped the pads over his elbows and knees, and pulled on his safety gloves. He could hardly wait to hit the ramps and rails!

He stood up and started forward. Suddenly, a hand grabbed him from behind and pulled him back.

"And just where do you think you're going?"

CHAPTER FIVE

Jonas whipped around. Bizz was holding his shoulder with one hand. In the other were two hockey sticks.

"Where do you *think* I'm going?" Jonas pointed to the ramps. "It's time for some action!"

Bizz handed him the stick. "It's time for action, all right — roller-hockey action! You *do* have your mouth guard, right?" Jonas nodded. "Well, then, come on! Everybody's waiting!"

X, Charlie, Mark, and Savannah were already at the roller-hockey rink. After Bizz and Jonas joined them, they chose sides for a three-on-three contest, took up positions, and started the game. They were no more than five minutes into it, however, when a familiar voice stopped them.

"Well, if it isn't the loo-oo-sers!" drawled a boy named Frank. He was straddling a mountain bike. Behind him stood three other boys, also on bikes. "What are you doing on *my* rink?"

Last fall, Frank and his team had challenged Jonas and his friends to a game of roller hockey. Both teams had agreed that the winners would have the right to use the rink whenever they wanted, regardless of who was there first. Frank's team had won the game — and now they could kick Jonas and his friends off at any time.

"C'mon, guys, let's get out of here," Jonas muttered. He started to leave.

"Whoa, whoa, whoa, no need to rush!" Frank said. "I'm not quite ready to jump on the rink." With a smirk, he hopped off his bike, hooked a chain through a link in the fence, and snapped a bike lock shut. "There! Okay, now I'm ready! Bye-bye, loo-oo-sers!"

Jonas felt frustration well up inside of him. But he tried not to let it show as he skated past Frank and his friends.

"Well, guess hockey's out for today," Mark said. "How about the ramps?" Jonas nodded, but the others headed for the rails. When Jonas saw the line of kids waiting for their turn on the half-pipe, he wished he'd gone to the rails, too.

The line moved slowly, but Jonas finally got his turn. Heart beating fast with anticipation, he steadied himself on the edge of the deck, then dropped down into the curve of the half-pipe. Wind rushed past his ears as he swooped down one side, did a one-eighty turn, and zipped up the other side. He went back and forth a few times, then his turn was over.

Mark finished a moment later. "Wanna go again?" he asked.

Jonas shook his head. He loved the half-pipe, but the thought of waiting another twenty minutes for less than a minute of action didn't seem that appealing. "I'm taking a snack break," he said.

Mark shrugged and lined up for another turn. Jonas skated to a bench and took out a pack of cookies. Suddenly, a fat raindrop landed on his nose. A moment later, the skies opened up and it began to pour.

Jonas shoved the last cookie into his mouth and unsnapped his inlines. The heavy rain made it hard for him to put on his sneakers, and by the time he got the second one tied, the park was practically empty. As he got up to leave, he spied Charlie and X skating toward the park exit.

"Wait!" Jonas called, hurrying after them. But they had already disappeared into the pounding rain.

"It's just a little rainstorm!" Jonas yelled. "Come back!"

CHAPTER SIX

"Rats!"

It had taken Jonas another five minutes to get to his bike, unlock it, and adjust the pack on his back. Now, as he navigated through the rain, wet spray shot up from the back wheel, dousing the seat of his pants. He was sure he'd be soaked through by the time he reached home. Then, as suddenly as it had started, the storm cleared up, and the sun was peeking out by the time he reached his neighborhood.

Figures, Jonas thought. *Stupid April showers. They stick around just long enough to turn everything to mud.*

He turned a corner. The mountain had been to his

left most of the ride home. Now it was directly in front of him. Jonas slowed to a stop.

Not that mud's always a bad thing, he thought, gazing up. He stared at the mountain for a moment, thinking. Then he checked his watch. It was twenty minutes to twelve.

Plenty of time for a quick ride over to the mountain. He pushed down on his pedals. *In fact, I probably should go to make sure the rain didn't wash away the sign Alison put up.* He pedaled faster.

Fifteen minutes later, he reached the trailhead. Alison's sign was posted nearby: TRAILS IN NEED OF REPAIR. PLEASE STAY OFF UNTIL FURTHER NOTICE — THANK YOU. He wiggled it. It was a little loose but otherwise seemed fine. He lingered for a moment, staring longingly at the trailhead. Then, with a sigh, he hurried over to his bike and got ready to leave.

"Yeee-haw!"

A loud shout echoed down the mountain. It was closely followed by another and then by a sound like branches breaking. Surprised and curious, Jonas wheeled his bike back to the trailhead. That's when he saw, in the muddy ground at his feet, a set of freshly made bike tracks. Someone was biking on the trails!

Jonas's first thought was to ride to the Community Center to tell Alison. But as he threw a leg over his bike, he heard another triumphant yell and loud laughter. Whoever was on the trails was having a great time. He paused.

You could be having a great time, too, a small, sly voice inside him whispered. *No one would ever have to know. And after the morning you just had, don't you deserve it? Besides, someone else has already ignored Alison's sign. What harm can it do if you ignore it, too?*

Jonas turned his gaze to Alison's sign. The front was white with black letters. Slowly, he reached forward, grabbed the sign, and twisted it around. The back of the sign was unpainted. It blended perfectly against the dark-green pine trees. Unless you were looking for it, you'd never know it was there.

I can always say I didn't see the sign, Jonas told himself. His mind made up, he took off his heavy backpack and hid it behind a rock. Then, with one last glance over his shoulder to be sure no one was watching, he mounted his bike, shoved off with one foot, and rode onto the tree-darkened trail.

CHAPTER SEVEN

The trail Jonas chose snaked back and forth, leading him up the mountain slowly. The incline wasn't that steep, but it was steady. He was forced to shift down to the lowest gear in order to keep moving. Even then he had to stand up and pedal in spots.

As he gradually made his way up the path, he wondered if he'd run into the other bikers. But when he stopped to take a drink, all he heard was rain water dripping off the trees. He realized he was on the mountain by himself.

Maybe I should head back, he thought, suddenly feeling uneasy. He glanced at his watch and saw that he'd been biking for twenty minutes. It would take him only half that much time to get back down. If he turned around now, the ride would be over before it had even begun.

He returned his water bottle to its carrier and began pedaling up the trail again.

It took him twenty more minutes to reach the top. By then, his legs were burning and he was breathing hard. He gulped some more water and looked over his shoulder down the winding path. His uneasiness returned.

He'd biked this trail many times before, but never so early in the season. Nothing looked familiar. The trees, many still bare of leaves, were wet from the rain and looked like black skeletons. Boulders he was sure he'd ridden by countless times seemed more jagged than he'd remembered. Murky puddles dotted the path.

There was no turning back, though, not unless he wanted to walk his bike all the way to the bottom. A quick glance at his watch told him he didn't have time for that, not if he was going to get home in time to do the chores his father had left for him. If he didn't get the chores done, his father would want to know what he'd been doing instead. With a stab of guilt, Jonas realized that he didn't want to have to answer questions like that.

So he took a deep breath, gripped his handlebars, and shoved off.

At first, he feathered his brakes, applying light pressure to keep from descending too fast. He shifted his weight to his rear tire, too, remembering that he was less likely to flip over his handlebars in that position. When the ride got bumpy, he stood up and let his legs absorb the worst shocks.

Slowly but surely, he began to get a feel for the trail. He relaxed his grip on the brakes and started to gain speed. He spied a tree root sticking up in the path, pulled back on the handlebars, and jumped his bike over it. With a grin, he twisted around a sharp curve and took the next straightaway at full tilt. When he spotted a small puddle in the middle of the trail, he aimed for it, whooping with glee.

The puddle was much deeper than it looked. Instead of splashing through it easily, his front tire hit the hole with so much force that Jonas's teeth rattled and he lost his grip on the handlebars. Arms wheeling, he flew backward and landed with dull thud at the foot of a pine tree. The bike skidded sideways, leaving a shallow rut in the soft mud before crashing into the brush.

Jonas lay on his back, stunned. After a minute, he sat up and examined himself gingerly. He was covered with muddy leaves and pine needles, and he could feel the beginnings of some bruises. But other than that, he seemed unhurt.

He got to his feet and walked over to where his bike had toppled over, certain he'd find a crumpled heap of metal and rubber. But when he set the bike upright and gave it a quick once-over, he discovered that it looked fine.

He took a deep, shaky breath and sat down next to his bike. "Wow, am I lucky," he whispered to the trees. And as he reached for his water bottle, it hit

him full force just *how* lucky he was: There was no one else on the mountain. His bike could have been broken apart into a million pieces. He could have been thrown against the pine tree. A sudden image of himself laying in the woods, unconscious and bleeding as the sun slowly set, flashed through his brain. It was followed by another picture of his father frantically searching for his only son.

And he wouldn't know where to look, because no one knows I'm here!

CHAPTER EIGHT

Jonas no longer cared how much time it took him to get down the mountain. He just wanted to get home safely. So instead of climbing back onto his bike, he walked it the rest of the way down. Only after he emerged at the parking lot and retrieved his backpack did he start to ride again.

He was halfway home when he realized something was wrong. His bike chain was catching every time he pedaled. He didn't have time to examine it, though — his watch told him it was already two o'clock. He had only an hour to do a full list of chores before his father returned.

At home, he stowed his muddy bike in the garage,

promising himself he'd clean it and check the chain right after he finished the housework. But when he read the list his father had left him, he groaned.

I'm supposed to empty the dishwasher, tidy up my bedroom and the basement, take out the trash, and vacuum the whole downstairs? he thought as he changed out of his rain- and mud-soaked clothes. *That'll take forever!*

It didn't take forever, but it did take most of the hour. When he finally finished, all he wanted to do was flop on the sofa and watch television. Then he remembered that he still hadn't taken care of his bike. With a sigh, he went out to the garage. His bike was right where he'd left it — but he was shocked by how bad it looked.

While he'd been cleaning the house, the mud splotches on the frame had dried, leaving the bike covered in flaky dirt. The paint had new scratches on it that Jonas hadn't noticed earlier. And he saw that the reflector from his back wheel was missing.

Jonas realized once again just how lucky he'd

been to walk away from his fall with only a few bruises. He returned to the kitchen to get some clean rags. But before he could find any, he heard the garage door open and a car drive in.

"Hey, Jonas!" he heard his father call. "I hope you got those chores done, because I have some plans for us this afternoon!"

Mr. Malloy entered the kitchen a moment later. He was holding two tickets. "They're for that skateboard movie you've been dying to see," he announced. "Show starts in twenty minutes. We'll grab a bite to eat after that, okay?"

Jonas hesitated, his thoughts on his bike. If he went with his dad, he might not get to it until the next day. But he couldn't very well tell his father that he needed to clean his bike instead of going to the movies. His father would want to know why it was so urgent, and he might even want to see the bike!

As it turned out, his father solved the problem for him.

"Did you get caught in that rainstorm on the way

home?" Mr. Malloy asked. "There were some pretty big puddles." He pointed to his feet. "I stepped in one. Soaked my shoe straight through to my sock!"

"Yeah," Jonas said. "I, um, I rode my bike to the park, you know. It got pretty wet on the ride back." He looked toward the garage. "In fact, I should probably clean it up."

Mr. Malloy checked his watch. "You've got ten minutes. But that should be enough, right? After all, it was just a little rainwater. A quick wipe down should do it."

"Uh, right," Jonas replied, wondering how much dirt he could clear off in that short amount of time.

Just then, the phone rang. Jonas answered. It was Alison.

"Jonas, I'm calling to tell you I'll have a surprise for you at the mountain tomorrow."

Jonas had almost forgotten about the mountain cleanup scheduled for the next day. "Surprise? What kind of surprise?"

"I'll give you a hint. Right after the rain stopped,

someone called to say they spotted a biker going up the mountain."

Jonas's heart stopped. "Oh, yeah?" he managed to squeak.

"Yeah," Alison said. "And my surprise has everything to do with that biker. Well, see you tomorrow."

Jonas slowly put the phone back in its cradle. He felt numb. He knew he was the biker she was talking about. He dreaded finding out what her "surprise" might be.

"All set to go?" Mr. Malloy asked, coming down the stairs. Jonas just nodded. It wasn't until they were pulling out of the garage that he remembered he hadn't taken care of his bike.

Not that it matters, he thought dismally. *Dad will find out tomorrow that I was on the mountain alone. And when he does, it's good-bye, biking. . . .*

CHAPTER NINE

Jonas slept poorly that night. The next morning, all he wanted to do was stay under the covers. Instead, he got up and dressed in long sleeves and pants.

"You're awfully quiet," his father commented over breakfast.

Jonas shrugged. "Just thinking about the cleanup, I guess," he mumbled, pushing his cereal bowl away and heading to the garage. "I'll meet you in the car."

Mr. Malloy followed him. "Don't you want to ride our bikes over?"

"Might as well," Jonas replied, adding silently, *since it may be the last time I ride for a while.*

When he wheeled his bike, still covered in dirt, away from the wall, Mr. Malloy's eyebrows shot up. "That must have been some puddle you rode through yesterday!" he exclaimed.

Jonas picked at a clod of dirt stuck to his handlebar. "It was," he said.

His father continued to stare at the bike, particularly at the back wheel. Then he looked at Jonas questioningly.

"C'mon, we better get going," Jonas said hurriedly, before his father could ask him about the mud. He mounted his bike and coasted down the driveway. Then he pushed off and started pedaling in the direction of the mountain.

Click. Click. Click.

For a moment Jonas couldn't figure out what he was hearing. Then he felt the hitch in his chain, the one he hadn't had time to check yesterday. With each push of the pedal, the clicking chain seemed to scold him. He wanted to stop and fix it, but that would mean facing his father. So instead he kept riding, hoping he wasn't making the problem worse — and praying that his father couldn't hear the clicks.

The rest of the clean-up crew was already in the parking lot when Jonas and his father rode in. As Jonas got off his bike, X hurried over to him.

"Look who's here," he said in a low voice.

Jonas glanced up and started. Frank and one of his friends were huddled against a boulder near the trailhead.

"What're they doing here?" he asked.

"They're the surprise I told you about," Alison said, joining them. She beckoned to Frank and his friend, who reluctantly came over. "That biker I told you about? It was Frank here. I caught him and his friend right as they were coming off the trail yesterday."

"Yeah, and then she forced us to show up here today!" Frank snapped. "Told us she'd ban us from the skatepark if we didn't repair the damage we did yesterday."

"You got that right!" Alison retorted. "You should

44

see the huge ruts they left. And not only did they ignore my sign, they turned it around so no one else would see it!"

"We did not!" Frank replied hotly. "I mean, yeah, we went on a trail, but we didn't touch your stupid sign."

"Well, someone did. And if not you, then who?"

Jonas knew this was the moment he should speak up. Confess. Tell Alison and his father everything. But he hesitated — and then Alison called everyone together, and the moment passed.

However, the guilt he felt for deceiving his father and Alison, and for letting Frank and his friend take the blame, stayed with him.

CHAPTER TEN

The clean-up crew gathered at the trailhead. Some of them carried rakes; others had shovels. X's mother had a chain saw.

"Everybody got their work gloves on?" Alison asked. Everyone nodded. She turned to Frank. "We'll start with the trail you were on and branch out. You'll be repairing all the ruts you made."

For the next hour, the crew slowly made their way up the trail, removing rocks and cutting back branches. When they came to the ruts Frank and his friend had left, Alison handed Frank a shovel. Grumbling, Frank started leveling the dirt.

"Catch up to us when you're done," Alison said. "We'll be on the next trail over." She led the crew to a spot where their trail intersected with another. With a jolt, Jonas realized that the new trail was the one he'd been on the day before.

"Frank claimed they were only on that last trail," Alison said, "but I'm going to scout ahead and make sure."

As she vanished around a bend, Jonas started clearing rocks off the path. He'd been at it for only a few minutes when Alison returned, looking furious and clenching something in her fist.

"Frank, get over here!" she bellowed. The rest of the crew stopped what they were doing, curious.

Frank appeared a moment later. "What now?" he snapped.

"I was hoping you could explain why I just found another rut on a trail you *swore* you hadn't been on. And," she added, "I found this in the brush near the rut." She opened her hand to reveal a bright-red bike reflector.

Frank snorted. "That's not mine. Someone proba-bly lost it last year."

"Not a chance," Alison shot back. "It would have been buried in dirt and debris. Someone lost this re-cently."

"Well, it wasn't me!"

Alison's eyes blazed. "You lie to me again and I will *definitely* ban you from the skatepark!"

"He's not a liar. I am."

Jonas pushed his way through to Alison's side. He reached out and took the reflector from Alison's hand. "This is mine."

Alison stared. Frank smirked.

Jonas felt a heavy hand on his shoulder. "And what exactly is your reflector doing up here, Jonas?" his father asked. His voice was low, but Jonas could hear the anger in it.

Jonas swallowed hard. "I — I was up here yester-day. I had a wipeout. My reflector must have come off then." He turned to Alison. "And I was the one who turned the sign around."

"Told you I didn't do it," muttered Frank. Alison grabbed his arm and pulled him away. The rest of the crew backed off, too, leaving Jonas and his father alone.

"You mean to tell me you went mountain biking by yourself on trails you knew were unsafe?" Mr. Malloy asked. "Did anyone know you were up here?"

Jonas stared at the ground and shook his head.

Mr. Malloy let out a long breath. "And you had a wipeout. Well, that explains why your bike was such a mess this morning. And why your chain was clicking." Jonas's head snapped up. "Oh, yes, I heard it. And I noticed your reflector was missing. I figured you had lost it in the rainstorm yesterday." He shook his head. "It never crossed my mind that you'd been up here."

"I — I'm sorry, Dad," Jonas whispered.

Mr. Malloy knelt in front of his son. "Rules are made for a reason. One reason is to keep people safe." He sighed. "You know I have to punish you, right?"

Jonas nodded.

"I was looking forward to biking with you," his father said. "But I guess that will have to wait. No mountain biking for one month." He stood up. "Now, let's go take care of that rut you made."

As awful as the punishment was, Jonas knew it was fair. He also knew he'd learned a lesson he wasn't likely to forget. As he picked up a shovel and followed his father, he vowed that the next time he took a wild ride, he'd stick to the rules — and play it safe.

What Goes Up Must Come Down

Mountain biking is a two-part activity. Part one is going up the mountain. Part two is coming back down. Both require steady balance, strong legs, and quick reactions. But how one gets up a mountain is very different from how one gets down.

Riding your bike up a mountain means pedaling — hard. One way to make pedaling a little easier is to shift your bike into a lower gear. Another is to stand up in the seat so that you can use the full force of your leg muscles to push the pedals. Rocking the bike back and forth while standing helps keep you moving, too. To rock, lean your bike to the right as your right pedal pushes down, then to the left as your left pedal pushes down.

After all the hard work of making it up a mountain, coming down may seem like a piece of cake. But descending takes just as much, if not more, concentration and effort as the climb. For one thing, riders need to control their speed. Since jamming on the brakes while careening down a hill could cause you to flip over your handlebars, keep forward momentum in check by squeezing the brakes lightly over and over instead. This is called feathering.

Taking corners while coming down a hill can be tricky. To corner safely, brake before you start to turn. That way, you're less likely to lose control. Leaning into a turn can help keep you stable, too. And keep your eyes on the trail! The brain has a way of telling the rest of the body to follow where the eyes lead. If you're looking somewhere else, you may steer your bike off the trail without even knowing it.

On your way down the mountain, you're likely to run into obstacles such as fallen branches, roots, rocks, and holes. If you're a beginner, your best bet is to swerve around them if you can. If you can't, shift your weight backward so that your front wheel can pass over the obstacle more easily. Since the front wheel is connected to the handlebars, riders can lose control of the bike if the front wheel hits something hard enough.

More advanced riders can loft or bunny hop — lift the front or the front and back wheels — over obstacles. However, these moves take weeks to master. To learn how to do these and other moves, join a mountain-biking club, pair up with an experienced rider, or research these techniques at your local library. But before you attempt any of them on a trail, be sure to practice, practice, practice!